MW01042215

Clint Cowboy

Book 2

The Cowboy Ranch Series

written by:

Kim Anderson Stone

Cover Photo: Kim Stone Photography

Edited by: Lindsay Boone

This book was created from very special memories of time spent with my children and grandchildren.

There are many people to thank for the love and support given to me during the writing of these stories. This book is dedicated to our grandchildren: Cole, Jay, Jessie, Madison, Luke, Cohen, Kyler, and Kinsley....and we aren't through yet!!

A very special thanks to my Dad and Mom.

Clint Cowboy

The Cowboy Ranch Series

Chapter 1

The big yellow school bus rumbled to a stop at the cattle gap of The Cowboy Ranch. Three boys ran down the bus steps and headed towards the ranch house as the big bus turned around and headed back to town. Six-year-old Clint Cowboy was doing his best to keep up with his big brother, Cody, and Cody's best friend, Hank Welder.

The older boys were barely paying attention to the little guy. They were planning their weekend of camping out and fishing.

Now that they were 12, they thought they were grown. Clint was half running and dragging his book bag behind him, getting madder by the second. It wasn't fair that he was just 6. He'd be glad when he was 12. Cody and Hank could go camping by themselves, and he had to stay home and do his brother's chores.

There were all kinds of mean thoughts going on in that little blonde head as he struggled to keep up. Clint knew he wouldn't do any of the mean things he was thinking of, but right now he was busy thinking them anyway.

Otis, the big White English bulldog, barreled out of the yard and headed straight for Cody. Every day the dog ran out to meet his boys. He loved his boys. Today, the big dog jumped right before he got to Cody. Cody was so busy talking to Hank that he never saw it coming, and the force landed him right on his britches. Clint had to giggle a little. Maybe he didn't need to think all those mean thoughts after all.

After a few minutes of rolling around with Otis, Cody and Hank went on their way. Clint was left standing by himself. He was still feeling mighty sorry for himself when his old beagle waddled out to him. Gibbs sat his fat rump down on Clint's boot and let out a mournful boo-roo howl. Clint hugged the old dog close.

Otis was young and playful, but Old Gibbs was fat and worn out. Otis left Gibbs behind now. Clint reckoned he knew how the old dog felt. Clint could always count on Gibbs to be by his side. They made their way through the gate and up to the farmhouse, looking like it was the end of the world.

Clint came through the kitchen door and dropped his book bag in its place by the washroom. Mama Cowboy took one look at her little boy and knew something was wrong. That was the saddest face she had ever seen. She was pretty sure he wouldn't be upset for long once he looked over at the table! Clint pulled off his boots, hung his hat up on the peg, and looked up with big sorrowful blue eyes. Then he saw him!

"Grandpa!" Clint shouted as he took off across the kitchen. His best friend in the whole world was right here in his kitchen, and he'd have him all to himself because Cody was going camping. He went from sad to happy just like that.

Chapter 2

Clint climbed up in his grandpa's lap and started talking as fast as he could. "Grandpa, I'm so glad you came to see me. I have to do all of the chores 'cause Cody is going camping with Hank and they won't let me go 'cause they say I talk too much but I wouldn't talk too much out there 'cause I'm 6 now and I know how to be quiet. See?"

Clint shut his mouth tight and looked up at his Grandpa. The grownups busted out laughing. Clint just started laughing, too. He didn't know why he was laughing, but he was pretty sure if it was funny to Grandpa, then it was funny to him.

Clint loved his grandpa. He loved his grandma, too, but it was Grandpa who came out to the ranch to play with him. Grandma just sat in the house with Mama Cowboy and talked about cooking and stuff. Grandpa said that's what girls do, so it must be true. His grandpa was the smartest man he knew.

After having a snack of warm biscuits and honey, Clint needed to get started on the chores. Work on a ranch never ended. The animals had to be fed every day, even on the weekends. He was headed over to the door to put his boots back on when Cody and Hank came down the stairs carrying all of their camping gear. They hardly even slowed down as they tore through the kitchen and out the back door. Clint kind of wished they'd trip over their fishing poles. He sure was jealous.

Clint started out to the barn trying really hard not to think those mean thoughts. He felt his grandpa walk up beside him. Clint reached up to hold the old man's hand. His grandpa had big, strong hands that were rough and scarred from years of working as a carpenter. Somehow, holding on to that hand made Clint feel a little bit better. He looked up at his grandpa and did his best to smile.

Chapter 3

Grandpa cut the bales of hay open and opened the stall doors for Clint. They worked together without saying much and soon had the horses fed. They spent a little extra time with Boloney, the old black and white pony in the end stall. They gave him a good brushing and some extra hay. Boloney liked to get out of his stall and raid Mama Cowboy's garden, but today he was where he was supposed to be. Clint said, "Grandpa, Boloney's just 'chevious. He don't mean to be bad."

Before long, all of the animals were fed. Grandpa was putting up the last of the feed buckets when he noticed Clint wasn't beside him. He saw the little boy standing at the end of the barn, looking out towards the lake. Clint's shoulders drooped. He looked so sad.

The old man walked down to stand beside his grandson. Grandpa looked towards the lake and saw the reason for Clint's sad face. Down by the lake, Cody and Hank were busy fishing and laughing with each other. They had their tent set up and a fire blazing. They looked like they were having so much fun. No wonder little Clint was feeling so sad. Grandpa knew how it felt to be left out. Since he had gotten older, he couldn't get around like he use to.

Suddenly, an idea came to him. He may be old, but he bet he could still play a trick or two. Yes Sir. He had an idea! Grandpa reached down and knocked Clint's hat off his head and said, "Quit your pouting, boy. We have some planning to do!"

Clint grabbed his hat and put it back on his head. He had to run to catch up with his grandpa. Clint had never seen him walk so fast.

Grandpa stopped by the wood pile, picked out two small limbs, and carried them with him to the house. He made it as far as the porch swing and plopped down. He dug his pocket knife out and began to whittle away at the first limb.

Clint climbed up beside his grandpa and began to ask questions. "What are we making, Grandpa?" "What are our plans?" "Why are we on the porch?" "Why do you want me to be quiet?" "Why don't we want Mama and Grandma to hear us?" "Are we gonna get in trouble?" "Will Grandma whoop you, Grandpa?"

Grandpa did his best to keep up with Clint's questions. He told Clint his plans and laughed as the little boy realized what he was up to. They were still laughing when Daddy Cowboy came in from the fields. The two big men shook hands. Daddy Cowboy sat down in the rocking chair across from Grandpa and Clint and asked what was so funny.

That started Clint talking. Soon, Daddy Cowboy was in on the plans. He just wondered how he would keep Mama Cowboy and Grandma from skinning their hides.

Grandma came out on the porch to call the men in for supper. She saw them laughing and put her hands on her hips. "Grandpa, what are you up to? You better behave yourself! And clean up that mess you've made with your whittling."

Grandma and Grandpa sometimes fussed like two wet cats in a feed sack, but mostly it was all in fun. They had loved each other for over 50 years. After so many years, Grandma had learned that Grandpa was always up to a little mischief.

Chapter 4

The family went inside, washed up, and gathered around the table. Tonight, when Daddy Cowboy blessed the food, he added a special prayer for Cody and Hank to be safe down by the lake. Clint couldn't help himself. He snorted right out loud during the blessing. He just knew Daddy Cowboy would get him, but he just kept right on with the blessing.

When everyone said "Amen," Clint looked up and saw Mama Cowboy looking at him with her pretty green eyes. Clint knew that look. For the rest of the meal, Clint was on his very best behavior.

Mama Cowboy was a good cook, but tonight Clint thought the chicken and dumplings were extra good. He could only think of two reasons why they tasted better: First, he bet his grandma helped cook them, and second, he was eating them while Cody and Hank were eating cold biscuits. Every now and then, Grandpa would look over at Clint and give a little wink.

Clint was so excited that he finished his supper, thanked his mama and grandma for the meal, and said he was plumb wore out from the extra chores. He reckoned he would go on up and get a bath to go to bed.

Mama Cowboy jumped up from the table and felt Clint's head. She started kissing him and asking him if he felt ok. Clint never wanted to go to bed early, and he certainly didn't ever volunteer to take a bath!

Daddy Cowboy came to the rescue when he told Mama Cowboy that Clint had worked extra hard today and to let him rest and quit fussing over him. Clint shot up the stairs like a cat, fast as his little legs would carry him.

Chapter 5

While the women put away supper and cleaned up the kitchen, the men went back out to the porch. Grandpa went straight for the broom and began to sweep up his mess. He had learned a long time ago that what Grandma said, Grandma meant.

Grandpa put the broom away and headed for the swing, only to find Gibbs flat out on his side, snoring away, so Grandpa sat down in the other rocking chair instead.

He pulled the pieces of wood out of his jacket pocket and handed them over to Daddy Cowboy. He said, "You think you could spare a piece of old inner tube from a tire? I think these would make some fine sling shots. I think they'd shoot rocks all the way to the lake if we were to get just a little closer.

Daddy Cowboy went out to the barn and came back with two strips of the thick rubber. The men worked together, one holding the wood and the other tying the rubber in knots around the forked end.

Page 21

They had to make quick work of hiding them when Mama Cowboy brought scraps out to feed Otis and Gibbs.

Mama Cowboy asked where Otis was. "I sent him down to the lake to watch out for Cody and Hank," Daddy Cowboy said. Otis took his guard dog duties seriously. Grandpa hadn't thought of Otis when he came up with his plan. He'd have to think on that.

Grandma joined them on the porch. They spent the rest of the evening talking and laughing. Every now and then, they could hear the sound of Cody or Hank laugh.

Mama Cowboy felt a little sorry for Clint. There Cody was, laughing with his friend on his first camping trip, and her youngest boy was so worn out that he just went to bed.

She decided that she'd make Clint a big stack of blueberry flapjacks for breakfast. That was sure to make him smile.

Chapter 6

The moon was shining brightly when Grandpa and Daddy Cowboy announced it was time for bed and headed to their rooms. Mama and Daddy Cowboy had just settled in when they heard a noise outside. It sounded like something must have fallen on the porch!

Daddy Cowboy grabbed his britches and pulled them on. He tiptoed down the stairs, knowing exactly what the noise was, but he had to put on a show for Mama Cowboy. He eased out the back door and down the steps. Sure enough, he was just in time to see the shadow of an old man and a little boy sneaking out towards the lake.

Daddy Cowboy laughed to himself and headed back inside. He went back upstairs and said, "That Boloney. I swear that ol' pony could get out of anything. He didn't make it to your garden, though." Well, it was kind of the truth. Boloney could get out of anything, and he wasn't in the garden. Daddy Cowboy just left out the part about the noise not being the pony.

Chapter 7

Cody and Hank were feeling like real men. Their bellies were full of the fish they'd caught and cooked themselves over their campfire. They were leaned back on the rocks. Man, this was the life.

All of a sudden, Otis threw his head up, and a low rumble started in his chest. He jumped up, the hair on his back standing up as he looked towards the barn and growled.

Otis took off at a run, barking his guard dog bark, leaving Cody and Hank beside the fire. Cody looked at Hank. Hank's eyes were round as saucers as he stared into the darkness towards the direction Otis had headed.

They could hear Otis barking and growling something fierce. Then, all of a sudden, he stopped barking. Cody called to him, but Otis didn't come back. Cody called him again and again, but the big dog didn't come back.

Cody told Hank that Otis probably just went back to the house for his dinner. He felt sure he'd be back. Otis never disobeyed Daddy Cowboy.

They sat back down by the fire. Hank started telling Cody about the time he took Sarah Rose fishing in the creek by the church. Cody knew Hank liked the new little girl in town.

Sarah Rose sure was pretty, but Cody didn't even think he'd want to take a girl fishing, no matter how pretty she was. He'd rather take Clint fishing than a girl.

Chapter 8

WHACK! Both boys jumped as something hit the side of the tent. "What was that?" Hank asked. Cody said he didn't know. And where was Otis? Why wasn't he coming back? WHACK! This time, the sound came from beside the fire. The boys spun around, looking this way and that. All of a sudden, a scream sounded in the dark. "That's a wildcat!" both boys said at once.

Out in the dark, Grandpa and Clint did their best to not laugh out loud. Grandpa shot another rock towards the lake this time. Clint was busy feeding Otis and Gibbs the cookies that Grandpa had snitched out of the kitchen when they were sneaking out. It was Clint's job to keep Otis and Gibbs quiet. Cookies seemed to be doing the trick.

Grandpa threw back his head and made a screaming sound again. Clint just stared at him! How did he sound just like a wildcat? Clint had to put his face in his hands to keep from laughing too loud. Ol' Cody and Hank looked like girls running around the campfire. They were scared. This was the best night ever.

Clint and Grandpa were so busy trying not to laugh that they didn't hear Daddy Cowboy come up behind them. Both of them about jumped out of their skin when Daddy Cowboy said, "Boys, we are in big trouble." Seems that Grandma realized that Grandpa wasn't inside, and she went and woke up Mama Cowboy. How were they going to get out of this mess? "Well, if we are in trouble, we might as well make it worth our time," Grandpa said as he shot another rock towards the tent.

Chapter 9

Cody looked at Hank. They didn't know what to do. If they got in the tent, the wildcat could get them. If they ran to the barn, the wildcat could get them. If they high-tailed it to the house, why, they'd never live it down.

What could they do? Where was Otis? Cody knew that the big dog would never leave them unless something bad had happened. He decided to call him one more time. Man! He almost fell down when he heard the big dog running towards them. At least he hoped it was Otis and not that wildcat.

Otis jumped mid stride and landed right on Cody's chest, knocking him to the ground. Otis started licking Cody's face while his tail was going ninety to nothing. Cody had never been so glad to see his dog in his life. Hank Welder just sat down on the rocks. Otis went over to Hank and licked him right in the mouth. "Yuck!" Hank said, "Get your cookie breath away from me…"   Cookie breath?   Both boys looked at each other. At the same time they said, "Grandpa!"

Cody and Hank heard the laughter before they saw the three shadows coming towards them.   Daddy Cowboy was the first to come into the firelight. He was really trying hard not to smile as he asked them if everything was ok.

Grandpa came up next, with Clint dragging up the rear. Cody really wanted to be mad. He'd love to grab Clint and throw him in the lake, but he knew that all of this hadn't been Clint's idea. Besides, it was kind of funny now....now that they knew they were safe.

"We got you good, Cody! You was scared!" Clint said. Cody grabbed his little brother and hugged him tight. He may be a pain sometimes, but Cody loved his little brother.

Cody said, "Clint, I'm sorry I didn't bring you with us to camp. I was just excited. It was wrong of me to leave you out. Do you want to stay with us tonight?"

Clint took one look around the camp. Then he looked out into the dark night. He thought about wildcats and other critters that could be out in the fields.

He took his grandpa's hand and said, "Maybe next time, Cody. I don't want Grandpa to get in trouble by himself." He would never admit that he was a little bit scared of the dark.

Chapter 10

Daddy Cowboy looked back towards the ranch house and saw that the kitchen light was on. There was no way to get out of it. They were in trouble.

They might as well get it over with. Daddy Cowboy, Grandpa, and Clint gave Cody and Hank one last hug and turned towards the house. Otis turned around and lay down beside Cody. He was back on guard dog duty.

Cody and Hank sat back down by the campfire. They were laughing and teasing each other about being scared. That was a good trick Grandpa pulled on them.

Daddy Cowboy, Grandpa, and Clint heard them laughing as they made their way up the steps to the ranch house. They opened the back door and sheepishly stepped inside. There sat Mama Cowboy and Grandma at the table, waiting on them.

Grandma lit into Grandpa like a tornado. Grandpa couldn't get a word in edgewise. Clint tried to sneak up the stairs, but Mama Cowboy caught him by the shirt tail.

She did her best to look mad, but she just couldn't do it. She hugged Clint and just busted out laughing. Then Grandma started to laugh. Before long, everyone in the kitchen was laughing. That was some trick they had pulled.

Grandma went over to Grandpa and gave him a friendly little smack on the arm. "Old man, when are you going to grow up?" she asked. Grandpa said that he hoped he never would.

Clint gave a big yawn. He climbed up in his mama's lap and took her face in his little hands. "Mama, I sure am sorry I told a story tonight, but I had to so you wouldn't know what we was doing. Mama, Cody was so scared, and I thought Hank was going to cry. You should have been there, Mama. I know I shouldn't have sneaked out, but Grandpa said it was ok just this time. Please don't whoop Grandpa, Grandma. He was just funnin' with Cody and Hank. We didn't hurt them," Clint said.

Grandma reached over and took Clint's hand. She said, "Let's get you up to bed, Clint. You can tell me all about it while I tuck you in. I reckon your Grandpa is safe. I think he won't get a whoopin' this time."

Mama Cowboy looked at the two men still standing by the kitchen door. She told them they might as well sit down and have some coffee. She said, "I had some cookies I could give you, but it seems that they just disappeared." With that, they all started laughing again.

Yes sir! It had been a good day on The Cowboy Ranch. It was late, and morning would be coming soon, but, for right now, the family was together laughing. There was no place on earth they'd rather be than right here on The Cowboy Ranch.

45695026R00027

Made in the USA
San Bernardino, CA
14 February 2017